One Bloody Night
The Austral Witches

Taila Cantrell

Contents

Dedication

To the spooky bitches who want to be fucked so hard it borders on abuse.

Trigger Warnings

Welcome Reader, to the darker corner of my smutty, dirty mind. Be warned before you go forward there be triggers ahead. That list will include:

Dubious Consent

Blood Play

Knife Play

Mild Stalking

Murder

Branding

BDSM. Keep in mind that this is a work of fiction, if you are going to practice any form of BDSM do your research on how to practice safely.

One

October 31st

8am

It's too fucking early to be naked in a field. I know that, but at least the wind is only a mild chill. At least Georgia didn't get cold until closer to Christmas. I felt around for my clothes, finally forcing myself to sit up. I tried to brush some of the leaves out of my hair, but realized it was a losing battle. There was no sign of clothes or any of my things surrounding me. I racked my brain, trying to figure out exactly how I ended up in this field. It wasn't familiar to me. Finally, my mind produced a single image of my grandmother bent over my bed, a grin on her face moments before I blacked out. I sighed, I should have known she'd trick me.

It was Halloween, one of my favorite nights of the year. Not just because it was my birthday. On Halloween, you could be anyone. Or better yet, do anyone. I shook away the horny thought. I had more important things to figure out. If grandmama had drugged me and left me out here, then she'd decided not to delay my Blood Rite. I stood, stretching my aching limbs. Leaving me naked was just unnecessary, she could have at least left me with a robe to wear. I glanced around, walking slowly, until I finally saw the road. I took a deep breath; I was going to have to walk the road naked until

I found someone who was willing to give me a hand. Then I had to come up with a plan on how I was going to complete the Blood Rite. This was not what I had planned for the day, but excitement still coursed through me. I was going to ascend today.

October 31st

8:37AM

I had been walking for what felt like forever. There were no houses or cars on the road in this area. My feet were aching. I cursed my grandmother silently for this. I should have been used to it. I was the only granddaughter of the Blood Coven's Priestess. There were no more women in my line to take over the coven. Grandmama tested my mettle every chance she had since I turned five and started showing signs of magic. Just little things at first, cats loved me, thunder when I was throwing a tantrum, the occasional floating toy. I'd done my first spell at sixteen when my high school boyfriend dumped me for a cheerleader. Grandmama had gotten quite a laugh when he turned up to school with no hair and a face full of acne. The whispers around school had made me second guess that spell. Too many sneering faces called me a witch. Just because it was true didn't mean it didn't hurt. Humans can't handle the reality of what lives among them. The wind cut against my naked skin, pulling me out of my thoughts, reminding me that I was alone and naked on a country backroad with no money. I mentally flipped through my grimoire. I knew it sat on my bedside table, just a few spells lined its pages. Grandmama had given it to me on my twenty-first birthday. Every witch or warlock had a personal grimoire, gifted to them by a family or coven member. Of course, the coven and head families had a large one that was passed down to the Priests. It was an honor to have a personal spell added to the coven's grimoire. That was my goal. One day I would be the Priestess of the Blood Witches, my spells would live on long after I was dust in the wind.

The sound of an approaching motor had me whipping around, praying that some kind person would stop to assist me. When an old black beat up Chevy truck came sputtering to a stop a few feet in front of me, I didn't breathe a sigh of relief.

"Darlin' are you aware you ain't got not a stitch of clothing on?" The Southern accent of the man sitting in the driver's seat caressed my ears. I took him in, a full dark red beard covered half of his face, his matching red hair was cut short, just enough that I could imagine running my fingers through it. He was handsome in a rugged sort of way.

"Yes, sir I am. It seems my night got a little out of hand." I sauntered toward him, watching as his hazel eyes roved over my body.

"Indeed, it does. My home ain't too far from here. You can call for some help there." He offered, motioning for me to climb in the truck. The leather seats were worn, cupping my naked ass in an obscene way. Once I was buckled in, he reached over giving me his hand, "Fang Boucher at your service ma'am."

"Bambi Cruor. I appreciate your help today." I replied, taking his hand. It was much larger than mine, and very warm.

"Bambi, the pleasure is all mine." I noticed a dark light in his eyes as he looked away. A shiver ran down my spine, but I ignored it. I was a badass witch, no man scared me.

Two

October 31st

9:17am

"Right through here, Miss Bambi. You can get cleaned up, here's a shirt to cover yourself with." Fang handed me a stack of towels and other things, a congenial smile on his face. I could see a predator in his eyes though, watching me closely. I forced myself to nod nervously, keeping any of my own predator out of my face. I didn't need this man to fear me. If he tried to harm me, I could defend myself. As he turned to walk out, I watched the muscles on his back, straining against the tight black shirt he was wearing. I'd love to see how the predator I'd seen in his eyes played with my own. Instead, I shook away my lust and stepped into an ice-cold shower. While I washed, I whispered a spell, sending my intention into the universe, shaping my words into reality. Soon my best friend would receive a raven with a message on exactly where to find me.

I was drying off my hair when I heard the bathroom door open, before I could turn a hand clamped over my mouth. I tried to speak, but Fang's voice in my ear stopped me, "Shh, shh Miss Bambi. I surely thought I smelled witch on you. I just couldn't believe my luck. You'd think it was my birthday."

I snorted under his hand, but he ignored me, "You ain't from around here, but you know the laws, girl. Any witch without a coven must report to the closest Priest before entering town. It seems you've broken some rules." He turned me so I could see him in the mirror, "Do you know what coven I belong to?" I shook my head as much as he'd allowed. Honestly, I hadn't gotten a hint that he was a warlock. I was stupid for forgetting to use my Other Sight. "I am a member of the Black Coven. Do you know what we practice." My breath hitched and I nodded, "Ah very good. Makes this easier. I was just leaving home to find a... participant in a spell I need to work. You'll do finely for that."

He moved his hand, giving me a chance to speak, "And if I refuse."

He didn't immediately respond, trailing his fingers over my collarbone, "You won't."

I hummed instead of responding. The Black Coven was well known throughout the state. The Blood Coven had been named with little imagination, we were known for the use of blood in our workings. We hunted the worst of humanity, tortured them, and used their blood for our spells until it was gone. I loved my coven, even if I had yet to be fully inducted, they had my heart. The Black Coven was different, instead of blood, they used the power of sexual energy to cast their spells. It was rumored they'd hold victims for days, draining every ounce of lust from their bodies until they were nothing but husks of their former selves.

"Will it kill me?" I asked.

He chuckled, "No. You'll enjoy yourself immensely."

I eyed him, looking for deception. I had a feeling even if I wanted to say no, he wouldn't like it. So, with a small shrug I gave him a nod. I wasn't prepared for the flurry of motion my agreement would create. Before I could think he had chained my hands above my head to the bar that held the shower curtain. My tits swung from the momentum he created, and I wasn't prepared when he slapped one of them gently. I gasped at the sensation, warmth flooding toward my core.

"Responsive." He muttered, fingers running down my body, probing me in various places, but careful not to touch anything too sensitive. When his hand ran down my thigh, I moved my legs earning me several slaps to my ass, "You'll stay still. Move only if you're told."

I glared at him, and he chuckled, "You're a little spit fire. Maybe when this is over, I can convince you to join up with my coven."

I bit my tongue, refusing to give him any information. As far as he could tell I was not coven claimed. At least I'd get to have this man take me before Larissa got here. It was the best birthday present I could give myself. Yes, I'd lose time to find my victim for the Blood Rite, but on Halloween night all the freaks would be out. It was still early in the day, and I was all tied up now.

Teeth sinking into my breast brought me back to my current predicament. He'd bitten me hard enough to draw just a little blood, and I watched in rapt attention as it slid down the globe of my breast. I could feel my own life energy within just that small drop, I wasn't prepared when I watched him bend his head down and lick it away. I forced myself not to move as my heart began beating in my clit.

"Are you going to actually do something or does the Black coven not live up to its name?" I taunted, bored of this game he was playing.

He met my eyes, fire burning in them as he reached up pinching both of my nipples, "Magic can't be rushed, girl."

"I'm all woman, Mr. Boucher." I shot back.

"That you are," He responded, before one of his hands roamed in between my legs, cupping my pussy. I couldn't stop my shiver as one of his fingers dipped inside of me. He pulled it out, sucking it into his mouth, "Mm, you taste like magic." I moaned, needing more of his touch, but he turned away. I stayed still, remembering his earlier warning. When he turned around wielding a sharp knife my heart jumped into my chest. "Shh, shh. I promise you'll enjoy it."

"That's just what a serial killer would say." I muttered.

I wasn't prepared for the series of slaps that alternated between my breasts and ass. "Your sass is not appreciated." He growled, "You'll be a good girl for me won't you?"

I nodded. It's like this man had read my mind and drug out my most taboo fantasies. If it wasn't so eerie I'd be completely into it. "If things get to be too much for you, say 'apple pie'. Do you understand?" I nodded again, unable to find my voice. "Say 'yes sir' when I ask you a question." He growled, slapping my ass again. I could feel the heat radiating off of my ass, but all it did was cause my pussy to get wetter.

"Yes sir." I said, forcing my voice into a ridiculously high pitch. He glared for a moment but decided to ignore it. He lifted the knife again, tracing it gently over the skin of my collarbone. Then he ran it between my breasts, applying enough pressure to draw a small line of blood. I expected to hate the feeling, but all it did was intensify my desire. When he reached the apex of my thighs, he pulled the knife away. Getting on his knees. I wasn't prepared for him to lift my legs onto his shoulders, so I yelped earning me several more slaps. I had to bite my lip to keep from screaming when his tongue made contact with my pussy. He lapped at my clit, driving me to the fastest orgasm of my life. I didn't even flinch when a cold, hard object pressed at my entrance. "Look at that good little slut. Letting me fuck her with my knife. I bet you can't wait until I fuck you with my cock." I groaned as he continued to torture my clit. A second orgasm rushed down my spine, the scream that ripped from my lips foreign to my ears.

He pulled away from me completely, yanking his pants down. Before I could recover he pushed himself inside of me, causing me to shutter around him. Fang groaned, "So warm and tight. Like it was made just for me."

I gripped the handcuffs, lifting myself up slightly so I could drop back down onto his cock hard. He groaned again, "Gonna make me cum too fast." He panted. He wrapped his hand around my neck, cutting off my air slightly. I rolled my hips against him as he slowed down the pace. He took a deep breath, "Mother, Father, I call on you. Use the energy I provide to fuel the spell I work on your behalf." I only half listened as he spoke a series of ritual words. I was too dazed from my orgasms to figure out what kind of spell he was doing, but he'd promised I wouldn't be harmed so I chose to tune it out. He brought my attention back by pinching my clit. His lips pressed into my mine, demanding as his tongue plunged between my teeth. He fucked me harder, his thumb working me back into a frenzy. My orgasm once again crashed over me, but this time I felt his warm seed pump into me as well. Our screams joined as a dark purple light flashed around the room. I closed my eyes against its brightness.

I must have passed out for a moment, because the next thing I knew Fang had me in his arms, no longer cuffed. "Thank you, Miss Cruor. You did a fantastic job."

"Look at you. Manners after something like that." I chuckled as he carried me out of the room. I didn't pay much attention as he laid me on a soft bed, a warm blanket was pulled over my naked body. I dozed off to sleep, the most sated I'd ever been.

Three

October 31st

10:45am

A sound woke me from the deep sleep I'd found myself in. My body ached slightly, but it wasn't anything I couldn't handle. I looked around the darkened room, checking to see if Fang was anywhere to be found. When I realized I was alone, I pushed myself off the bed I'd been laid on, walking toward the window. When I pulled back the curtain I found the source of the noise. A jet-black raven hovered there, pecking its beak against the glass. I grinned, glancing down toward the driveway to see my best friend's bright pink car. I pulled a blanket around me, once again checking the room to ensure I could escape without notice. It was far too easy to open the window and slip down the trellis that adorned the side of the old house. When my bare feet hit the ground, I took off at a run, sliding into the passenger seat of Rissa's car in seconds. "Drive."

"Mon ami, please a little patience. You've had me drive out to the middle of nowhere to save your naked ass." Her Cajun accent made deciphering her words difficult to my Southern ears, but I'd known her ever since she moved up from Louisiana three years ago. I was used to it by now, "There's a sex crazed warlock in that house, Ris. We need to go."

"That don't sound too bad to me." She laughed, as she threw the car into reverse and spun her wheels out of the driveway.

My heart didn't stop pounding until we were miles away. Finally, I turned to her, "Did you bring me clothes?" She motioned toward a brown paper bag in the back seat. I grinned, grabbing it.

I pulled out a black lacy body suit first, followed by leather pants. Black stilettos with red bottoms were the final item I pulled out, "Do you have some plan I'm not aware of?"

"It's your birthday. We have to celebrate, regardless of Grand-mama Cruor's plans." She responded, "Dress. I'm starving. We start with food."

I didn't argue, my stomach growling loudly at the mention of a meal. Putting on a body suit in a tiny sports car that is flying around the curvy back roads of the South is harder than I'd like to admit, but by the time Larissa pulled into a small diner I was dressed and feeling back to my normal self. I glanced toward my friend, taking in her outfit for the day. Her long locs were pulled up into an orange and black scarf around her head. She wore a flowing black skirt that showed off the white swirling tattoos she'd had done last year. They stood out against her dark skin, drawing your eyes to her thick thighs. The white shirt she wore covered the scars on her arms but still drew attention to her full breasts. If I wasn't straight, Larissa would have been my dream woman. "Quit your staring, girl. I need some eggs in my tummy. You dragged me right out of bed with this coven nonsense."

I chuckled, "You know you love me, Ris."

As we entered the small diner, every head swung toward us. I couldn't blame any of the men gawking, we made an intriguing and attractive pair. I scanned the faces, reaching my powers out to hunt for a dark soul, when none returned to me, I sighed. Finding a victim for my Blood Rite was going to be harder than I expected.

There were requirements in the Blood Rite: Innocent souls were never to be used in rituals, you must find and kill your victim alone, it must be done on All Hallow's Eve before the clock struck midnight,

Grandmama had hinted several times that she was going to put my Blood Rite off for a year, give me an extra year to study and prepare to join the coven. Obviously, she had been misleading me.

"What can I get for you ladies?" A chubby dark-haired woman asked, approaching our table with far more cheer than I would be able to muster if I had to work here.

"Give me an order of scrambled eggs and bacon. Black coffee to drink please, cher." Larissa's melodic voice seemed to entrance the waitress, who leaned closer as she wrote her order down.

I closed my eyes, activating my Other sight. I felt no surprise as I took in the shadows that caressed every inch of exposed skin on my friend. The first few times I'd seen it I'd jumped back in surprise. I'd never met another witch whose magic called to their preferred method so strongly. I glanced to the waitress, a shadow had wound its way around her neck.

I coughed slightly before forcing myself to order, "Can I get the French toast with strawberries and an orange juice?"

"Course darlin. I'll get that in for y'all right now." The shadow dislodged itself, floating back down to join its brethren wrapped around Larissa's wrist.

I glanced around the room. There weren't any other witches dining in today, but two human men drew my attention. Their auras looked like oil had been poured over them. A smirk curled up my lip, either one of them would be perfect for the Blood Rite. I was surprised my earlier perusal of the room hadn't spotted them. One of them turned and looked my way, giving me a wink that made my skin crawl. Instead of reacting I gave him a wide smile and turned my attention back to Larissa. "What exactly are your plans?" I asked.

She flashed me her beautiful, white smile before she said, "It's your birthday, girl. We are going to spend the day having fun. There's a festival that starts in a couple hours. Apparently, they've got a real fortune teller," She rolled her eyes, but I knew exactly where her mind was. Finding any witch who could truly read the future was rare, but a few did travel with carnivals to keep a low profile. "I've also heard about a party late tonight that seemed like the perfect spot— "

Before she could finish one of the men I'd spotted a few minutes before appeared, nearly shouting, "Ello there, pretty ladies. What brings y'all to our fine little town?"

Larissa rolled her eyes, inspecting her nails as if the man hadn't said a word. I loved her attitude to those she viewed as being below her. My best friend would take no shit from any man for any reason. I wish I could be more like her. Instead, I plastered a smile on my face and responded, "We're checking out the festival downtown."

"Tim and me'd be more than happy to show you ladies around." The grin on this man's face screamed predator, and not in the fun way. It was the perfect solution to my problem. Either of these men would make perfect sacrifices for the Blood Rite. If I let them accompany us to this festival, I could lure one of them away and perform the spell.

"I'd love that!" I cringed when I realized I had nearly shouted my response. I glanced toward Larissa, who only seemed mildly perturbed by my interruption of her plans, "But let us finish up our breakfast please. I need some girl time."

The man gave a small roll of his eyes, but seemed pleased, "At least give me your name before I go back to my coffee."

"Bambi. Bambi Cruor." I reached over, offering my hand. He gripped my fingers tightly, before turning my hand over to leave a sloppy wet kiss along the back.

"My pleasure, Miss Bambi. I'll be seeing you real soon." He said, before walking back to join his friend.

"Is there anywhere you go that men don't harass you?" Larissa asked, once the man was out of ear shot.

I considered her question. I had been getting tons of male attention since I was twelve or thirteen and my assets started to become obvious. "I guess I don't think about it much. If they cross the line, I just hex them." I finally respond, brushing it off.

Larissa grinned, "And that's why we're best friends."

We chatted casually for several minutes, catching up on coven gossip and events around town. Grandmama had dropped me off about fifty miles from where we lived. I was lucky Larissa had been awake to receive my message. Usually, she stayed up until the wee hours of the morning. She was a night owl like no other. I guess it made sense considering her magic.

"Here's your orders, ladies. Let me know if y'all need anything else." Our waitress said, placing our food in front of us. I dug in immediately, not even realizing how hungry I was until the food was before me. I hadn't considered how much the spell Fang cast truly drained my energy. I should have paid more attention to what he was actually doing, but as I began to try to remember what he'd been muttering only the feel of his hands on my skin came to mind. He'd been the best lay I'd had in years, maybe ever. I cringed. I was never going to see him again. I shouldn't feel sad about that fact, considering he'd basically held me captive to use my orgasms in his spells.

I was finished eating in record time, wiping my mouth carefully to ensure I hadn't gotten any food on my face. I stood, "I'm going to run to the little witch's room." I stepped into the bright, white bathroom. Thankfully it was clean. I did my business quickly, struggling back into the tight pants Rissa had provided me. I stood in front of the mirror for a long time after washing my hands. Staring into my own grey eyes, an unknown feeling creeping into my consciousness. I glanced around the room, the hairs on the back of my neck raised. When I looked back into the mirror I saw the shadow of antlers around my own head, causing me to stumble backward with a curse. I rushed out of the bathroom, sliding into my seat across from my friend out of breath. "We need to get out of here. Now."

"What happened?" Rage darkened her brown eyes. I glanced down seeing the way her fists curled on the table, shadows gathering as if ready to attack at any moment.

"I think that warlock is after me." I whispered as she threw several crumpled bills on the table. Her eyes widened, but she gave a sharp nod of her head.

Just before we made it to the door a man's voice rang out behind us, "You didn't forget about me did you, darlin."

I cursed under my breath, having forgotten about my perfect victim, "Of course not, hun. We've just got a small emergency to attend to before the festival. Can we meet you there?" The honey I poured into my voice was boosted by just a hint of my natural magic.

He looked dazed for just a moment, before giving me a big, toothy smile, "I understand these woman things, darlin. We'll see you there."

I gave him a small wave as I yanked Larissa out of the door, nearly jogging back to her car. I slid into her passenger seat, my hands shaking as I rested my head against the dashboard.

"What the fuck happened?" Larissa asked as she started the car.

I didn't even know how to explain what I saw. She'd probably think I was crazy. I had no real proof that Fang had stalked me to the diner. I just knew he was messing with me, angry that I'd disappeared. Our time together had been fun, but I couldn't risk him stopping me from completing the Blood Rite tonight. "Can we just get out of here?"

She looked at me for a moment, before nodding. She threw her car in reverse and peeled out of the parking lot, leaving a trail of dust behind her.

Four

October 31st

12:15 PM

Less than twelve hours until I had to have this fucking ritual done, and instead of luring a victim in I'm standing in a line of screaming ten-year-olds trying to get tickets to get into the festival. Larissa and I had tried to perform a small spell to hide me from Fang, but the strangest thing had happened. Male laughter still echoed in my ears.

"Cheer up, love. I have no doubt those guys will find us." Larissa said, bumping me with her hip.

I just grumbled in response, exhaustion weighing heavily as I looked around. I'd felt eyes on me several times since we'd rushed from the diner, but nothing as obvious as the antlers had happened again. I snorted when I considered why the shadowed antlers had appeared. It was a cheap shot at my name, but if I hadn't been so scared I probably would have laughed.

When we finally reached the front of the line, Larissa handed over her debit card, paying for both of our tickets, "I'll flip you some cash back when I get home. I can't believe Grandmama left me with no phone or money."

"Don't worry about it, I've got plenty of money." I still hadn't figured out exactly how that was the case, Larissa didn't have a job. She didn't even really work for the coven. My best friend was a mystery in more ways than one, "Plus, it's all part of your test. You have to use magic to survive until you've completed the Blood Rite."

"Does summoning you actually count?" I joked.

"The fact you managed a spell like that without your grimoire, or your full Mother blessed powers is extremely impressive." I glowed at her praise. Larissa was the second most powerful witch I knew. Only Grandmama had her beat, and she was the Priestess of our coven. If Larissa would actually initiate into the Blood Coven, she could easily surpass Grandmama and I both. "Stop worrying and focus on your task."

"Yes ma'am." I saluted her. She rolled her eyes before disappearing into the crowd. It would be easier for me to find my victim if I was alone.

I closed my eyes, once again switching to my Other sight. A rainbow of auras filled my vision. Children always had pure souls, so it was easy to spot the tell-tale oil slicked auras of the wicked in this crowd. Three women walked by, only one had the blackness floating around her, but I dismissed her as an option. I knew I would prefer to prey on men, usually their wickedness was more vile than a woman's. Honestly, I was all for women's wrongs. Sometimes a bad bitch had to do bad bitch things.

"Miss Bambi, there you are. Where is your little coco friend?" I growled at the way he referred to Larissa, but I forced myself to turn around with a smile.

"She's around here somewhere I'm sure... I'm sorry, sir. I never did catch your name." I said, changing the subject.

"Just call me, Mike, darlin." He looked me up and down, leering at my breasts, "Tim, why don't you go find Miss Bambi's friend. We'll go find us a nice, quiet place to sit."

Tim grunted but turned and left without argument. Mike grabbed my elbow and led me away from the crowds. I smiled to myself, shocked at how easy he was going to make the Blood Rite for me. Maybe I could be home before dinner time to actually celebrate my birthday the right way. I knew exactly what kind of man this was, yet I still wasn't prepared when he led me down an alley and suddenly slammed my back against a makeshift wall.

"You're just too pretty for your own good, aren't you? Dressed like that how could any man resist you?" He clumsily slammed his lips to mine, causing me to flinch from the taste of tobacco and meat.

I kept my body relaxed, allowing him a few moments of fumbling groping. Just as he tried to slip a hand down my pants his weight lifted off of me. I blinked as his body hung in mid air for a moment.

"I don't like it when other people play with my toys." Fang's dark voice rang all around me. I froze, unsure what to do. Mike hung in the air, clutching at his throat, but not making a sound. I swung my head to the right, finding Fang staring at me, his grey eyes boring into me, "I'll take care of this for you." I heard the crack of Mike's neck just before he dropped to a heap on the ground.

I sighed, "You're really fucking up my day, ya know that?"

Fang furrowed his eyebrows, "That man was assaulting you ten feet away from a group of high school girls and I'm fucking up your day?"

"Look, I had fun and all, but I've got some stuff going on. You got your spell done, didn't you?" I asked.

"Yes..." I'd never seen a man look more confused. If I wasn't so annoyed with him it would be very cute.

"Okay, then I need you to leave me the fuck alone. It was a good lay, but come on, stalking me all over town." I said, turning to look at Mike's body, "And what are you planning to do about that?"

"Who the fuck are you?" Fang stormed toward me, "I've never seen an uncovened witch behave this way."

"Because I'm not uncovened dumbass. Today is my twenty fifth birthday, and you just interrupted me as I was just about to begin the ritual I need to do to join my coven officially." I snapped at him.

"You're only twenty-five." He looked horrified as he took me in. I understood what he was thinking. It was uncommon for a fully-fledged warlock to become involved with a young witch, frowned upon even. "What coven are you joining?"

"My grandmother is the Priestess of the Blood Coven." I said, bending down to rummage through Mike's pockets until I found his wallet.

"Fuck. Fuck of course..." He stopped, watching as I took all of the cash from his victim's wallet, "Listen we have a problem- "

"No sir. You have a problem. A body to clean up too. I've got to go." I started to stomp away, but Fang grabbed me.

I slammed my foot down on his, but he still managed to hold onto me, "I told you. You are mine now."

I didn't have time for his male posturing, so I called a spell to the front of my mind. I muttered the words quickly. Watching as Fang leaped away, his hand smoking, "I am my own." I said, before rushing away.

I was breathing hard when I finally found Larissa, "We gotta go."

"Again?" She sighed, glancing to her quickly melting ice cream. I nodded instead of responding, grabbing her free hand and yanking her along. "Slow down. My legs aren't as long as yours." She complained.

Once we were safely out of earshot of anyone at the festival, I let her go. "He showed up. He killed Mike from the diner for touching me— "

"That's kind of hot." Larissa interrupted me.

"True, but irrevelant. He said that I'm his. We need to get out of here. I'm not even sure where to go find a new victim now." I ran my hand over my hair, trying to catch my breath.

"Now we're going to go shopping. That'll help you calm down, then we can worry about how to find what you're looking for. You have plenty of time." She said, patting my back gently.

"I guess. Shopping does sound nice." I agreed.

She gave me a bright smile, before leading me away from the festival.

Five

October 31st
2:45PM

This little town, which I had yet to take the time to learn the name of, was absolutely full of the most adorable small businesses. I sighed as we walked out of another boutique. The fall air was a welcome breeze across my heated face. We'd been walking and shopping for a couple of hours. It had helped get my mind off of the unexpected events at the festival. Fang hadn't made any further appearances so hopefully he'd gotten the message. The only problem is I hadn't run across anyone else in town that would make a good victim for my Blood Rite. I was trying not to get frustrated, but I only had eight hours to find, lure in, and finally complete the ritual.

"The pouty look does suit you; I can't lie but come on babe. Stop stressing. It's all going to work out." Larissa said as she dragged me into the next store.

"Thanks for coming in ladies. Are y'all looking for anythin' in particular?" A chipper voice greeted us.

"Just browsing." We both responded, beelining to the Halloween costume display.

"This could work." Larissa held up a short red dress with a matching black cape.

"A little too on the nose for me." I wrinkled my nose, shuffling through the ridiculous sexy nurse or maid costumes. "What if I don't even find a party to attend?" I muttered.

"We'll find something to do." Larissa dismissed me.

"Oh, are you ladies looking for some events around town? I know there's a big barbecue over off Main Street." The sale's woman said, appearing from nowhere.

"You know of anything more intimate?" Larissa asked.

The woman tapped her chin, "If you're looking for a more adult crowd. There's a club over off Central Avenue. I think their event starts at five. It'll be going on all night."

"What's the name of the club?" I asked, intrigued.

"Rubies. It's a pretty popular spot. You'll probably want to get over there as early as possible if you want a table." She answered, before flouncing away without another word.

"And there's your perfect solution. Now we can focus on just shopping," Larissa said with a clap of her hands.

I grinned. She was right, I could relax now. A place like that would have plenty of options for my prey, all of them easy to lure in. The tension in my body eased as I browsed through the limited costume selection. I was just about to give up, when a green shimmer caught my eye. I pulled the dress out of the rack and nearly squealed. It was a perfect replica of a Tinkerbell outfit, shimmery white wings included. "I have to have this." I turned, showing the dress to Rissa.

She turned her head, shouting, "Do you have shoes to match this?"

The woman popped her head out of the back, catching a glimpse of the dress before disappearing again. I furrowed my brows, "I guess I can just wear what I have on."

Before Larissa could respond, she turned a pair of strappy, green heels hanging off her finger, "I've got one pair in a size six."

"Let me try them on," I reached for them, already preparing the spell to force them to grow to the correct size. By the time I had sat to remove my heel, the spell was already working it's magick. I slid my foot into the shoe, grinning as my size nine foot fit in them perfectly. "I'll take em." As the sale's associate walked away to package our purchases I muttered, "I love being a witch."

I glanced at Larissa, seeing an odd strain around her eyes as she smiled at me. "It's certainly convenient." She replied noncommittally.

"You okay?" I asked.

She shook her head slightly, the tension on her face melting away, "Just getting peckish. Want to grab some lunch?"

"Always." I smiled. I wouldn't press her further, but I knew when my best friend was suffering.

October 31st
3:22PM

"You're feeding me too well, Ris. I may never find a man at this rate." I groaned after taking the most delicious bite of a burrito I'd ever had. Juice dripped down my hand, but I didn't care as I took another bite.

"I don't think finding a man is an issue for you, Bams. More like keeping them away. Which I'll be honest, the queso on your mouth is probably doing a pretty good job." She responded, before handing me a napkin.

I sat my burger down reluctantly, wiping my face and hands, "We don't need men. We're strong independent witches." Larissa nodded along as I continued to rant about how awful men were. It wasn't that I was really a man hater, it just seemed like only the worst men crossed my path. As if summoned by the thought, Fang appeared on the sidewalk, catching my eye before storming toward us. I took the last bite of my burrito, before standing, "Why don't we go get changed so we can get over to Rubies early."

Larissa was still chewing but rushed after me as I went for the back exit of the restaurant. The streets were crowded with people shopping and socializing, so it was easy enough to get lost in the hustle and bustle. When I noticed a sign for public restrooms I dipped aside.

"Any reason why we rushed out of lunch?" Larissa panted.

"That fucking warlock showed up again." I cursed, after checking the stalls to make sure we were alone.

"Maybe you should just talk to him. I mean you did sleep with him; he can't be that awful." She reasoned.

"Traitor," I muttered. I considered her words; the sex had been exactly the kind I loved. Fang had been gentle and kind after the fact. Nothing like what I would have expected from a member of the Black coven.

"Cher, running all over this town trying to avoid a warlock is going to use up the time you need for a victim. If he shows up again, just have a quick chat with him." Larissa sighed, "Let's go ahead and get changed. Might as well start making our way toward this party."

Six

October 31st
5:13PM

The line was wrapped around the block. That sales associate hadn't given us a good enough idea on just how popular this place was. Thankfully, we had gotten here early enough that we should be inside in just a few minutes. I patted my hair slightly; the bun we'd wrestled it into was precarious and not my usual style. The rest of the outfit was perfect. The dress hit me mid-thigh, the strappy heels reached up my calf complimenting my long legs. I'd already gotten several compliments from men walking by. I glanced down at Larissa, who'd chosen a simple catsuit and ears. We hadn't had much makeup, but we'd managed to draw some whiskers on her face with eyeliner. She was pulling off the simple look as if it had been custom made for her.

"IDs." The girl at the door said, clearly bored. She was dressed as security, but with my Other sight I could tell she was a member of the Protection coven. I had planned ahead and used one of Larissa's old cards to look just like my driver's license. I extended it to the girl, hoping she wouldn't look at it with her Other sight. She waved us through without another word, and I sighed out a breath of relief.

I was shocked by just how many witches and warlocks were in attendance as we walked through the club. It was a nice place, the music wasn't overwhelming, and while there were definitely plenty of people dancing and grinding there were just as many people sat at tables enjoying each other's company. It was my kind of club, I wish I could actually enjoy the night instead of hunting down my prey. A few oil slicked auras stood out to me, but I knew I needed to let them approach me.

"I'm going to go dance. Are you okay on your own?" I asked Larissa.

"Go do you, girl. I'm going to grab a table and order myself a drink." She shouted. I waved at her as I made my way to the dance floor. It was easy to lose myself in the music, I didn't pay attention as I danced, letting my body graze the people around me. It felt good to let loose, so I closed my eyes, completely forgetting about all of my troubles. Songs changed, but I just kept dancing, hands ran over my body occasionally, but it never went too far. When one pair of hands became a little demanding, I turned. I looked up into a black mask, could see my greenish reflection in its shiny surface. The hands on my hips kept us swaying to the beat of the music. Something about the moment caused my pussy to clinch with neediness. I turned, grinding back against the masked man, feeling his erection press into my butt. A noise left my lips against my will, causing me to turn, grabbing his arm. I dragged the stranger off the dance floor, a single-minded focus to find a hidden, dark spot. I found a door leading into a dark hallway, ignoring the staff only sign I pushed ahead. When I found an unlocked supply closet I pushed the man inside.

I wasted no time, dropping to my knees before him. I fumbled for a moment in the dark, finding his belt buckle, and eventually freeing his cock. The masculine scent of him heated my core even further. I was desperate as I sucked his cock into my mouth, quickly working to press my nose to the base of him. He groaned as he felt my throat swallow around his girth. Suddenly, he wrapped a hand around my arm and yanked me to my feet. I was pressed with my face against the door in seconds, a hand cupping my bare pussy. The man growled, before quickly pressing inside of me. We groaned in unison. He felt huge as he pumped into me slowly at first, and then rougher until I couldn't stop the gasps and moans from falling from my lips. His hand suddenly wrapped around my mouth; I felt his mask pressing against my neck. I expected him to speak, but he stayed silent only a growl gracing my ears.

His other hand reached down, finding my clit and working it exactly how I liked. It was impossible not to grind back against him as he brought me to the edge of orgasm. He pulled away, causing me to scream into his hand in frustration. I heard a muffled chuckle before he pulled away from me completely, turning me around. He yanked my dress and bra down around my waist, caus-ing my breasts to spill out into his hands. He explored them slowly, causing me to writhe against the wall. "Please, just fuck me. I need to cum." I wasn't above begging if it got me what I wanted. He didn't move a muscle continuing to roll my nipples between his fingers. I growled in frustration, which apparently spurred him on, because he lifted me by my thighs, wrapping my long legs around his waist, and began fucking me harder than before. I dug my nails into his shoulders, groaning as he bumped against the perfect spot inside me. "Right there. Right there." He actually listened, continuing to pound into me exactly the same way. Within moments my orgasm was swelling and crashing over me. I heard his groan before I felt his warm seed spilling inside me. He held me there for a long moment, our panting breaths filling the small space.

He let me go gently, ensuring I had my feet under me. We righted our clothes in silence, just before I reached for the doorknob to leave, I said, "That was great. Thanks."

"Anything for you, darlin." I froze as Fang's voice touched my ears.

"You've got to be fucking kidding me." I turned, ripping the mask from his face. He didn't even have the wherewithal to look ashamed, "How dare you? If I'd known, it, was you— "

"I won't ever let another man touch you again." Fang growled, "Can you not feel the way our magics intermingle when we're together. If you— "

"I don't have time for this alpha male posturing bullshit," I screamed, "I have six hours to get my Blood Rite completed or I can't join the coven I've been training to become Priestess of since I was seven." He looked shocked as I poked my finger into his chest, "This is not how you tell a woman you like her."

"You're right," My eyebrows reached for my hairline at his admission, "Look Bambi. I don't do relationships. I'm barely involved with the Black coven. I prefer to be alone.... There's just something about you."

"I'm just a damn good lay." I said, feeling uncomfortable.

"I... feel something for you, I can't just let you go." He insisted.

"Fang, look... If you'll let me find my prey, we can... go from there. I have to do this. It's important to me." I couldn't lie to myself. There was something intriguing about the man standing before me. I didn't feel whatever he was saying about our magic, but he'd been on my mind all day. Not just because he'd stalked me all over town.

"I'm not leaving you alone on Halloween night." He growled.

I rolled my eyes, "Well make yourself scarce, because otherwise I'll never find someone to do the ritual." With those words I turned on my heel and stormed back into the club.

I beelined to the table where Larissa had become surrounded by several men, "'Scuse me, sir. Just trying to get a seat with my friend."

The guy glared at me for a moment until he took in my appearance. "Of course, ma'am. So sorry to be in your way. What's your name?"

"Bambi." I offered him, sitting next to Larissa, who pushed a bright red drink my way. I took a sip as I switched back to Other sight. All four of the men at the table were human, only one of them had an aura of interest. I turned my attention toward him, "And what's your name?"

He seemed surprised at my question, his blue eyes trailing down to my breasts before offering an answer, "Jacob."

"It's nice to meet you, Jacob. What brought you to our table?" I trailed the tips of my fingers over his arm as I spoke.

"Well, your friend here was telling my buddy, Eric, a story about her wrestling with a gator. When a tiny woman starts talking like that it piques my interest." He answered, scooting his chair closer to mine so our knees were touching.

"Oh, Ris would fight off a dragon if it pissed her off." I laughed genuinely.

"What about you?" He asked, getting bold enough to place a hand on my knee.

"I don't think I can claim to have ever fought a gator in the bayou, but I have my talents." I let my voice turn suggestive.

"Oh, I am sure that you do." Jacob grinned.

I took a sip of my drink to hide my own grin. Sometimes men were just too easy.

Seven

October 31st

7:42PM

I was bored. Listening to Jacob and his friend Eric drone on and on about their lives in this bar was going to be the death of me. At this point, they deserved what was coming for them just for making my eyes water from sheer boredom.

"Why don't we get out of here? We could go check out the haunted house over at the old Mills place." Eric said, an arm thrown around Larissa's shoulders. She sent me a withering look. I appreciated that she had put up with a guy all night, I could smell his BO from here. I'd find a way to pay her back for all her trouble soon.

"That sounds like a great idea." I smiled, allowing them to lead us out of the club. I'd have to come back here sometime and actually enjoy it.

The Mills place was not what I expected. The house was actually spooky, enough so that I immediately switched to my Other sight. I wasn't shocked to find the house coated in magic, shadows danced around, flickering white lights floated around the doorway. I glanced at Larissa, who reached for my hand. A confirmation she was seeing the same thing I was. Was the house actually haunted? The people walking out looked genuinely disturbed. "Are you guys sure this is a good idea?" I heard myself asking.

The guys ignored me completely, marching toward the front of the line to enter the house. Only one person stood there. A grim look on his face as Fang turned to meet my eyes. I almost stormed up to him, but I realized no one else knew who he was. These guys wouldn't take well to my telling off some random guy for no reason. So, when we reached him, I refused to meet his eyes again.

"Welcome to the Mills Place. Tonight, the Panther's theater kids are here to give you all a fright." A bored teen appeared, moving the velvet rope to allow us in, "Any injuries to the actors are met with serious consequences. We're not responsible for any harm that might come to you. Enjoy the screams." He stopped just outside a room with fake fog filling the doorway. "Begin here."

"Don't worry, babe. You can hold my hand." Jacob said, an arm wrapping around my waist. I couldn't help cutting my eyes toward Fang as the man touched me. He wasn't looking, but the muscle in his jaw was ticking. Something about that made me want to climb on top of him in the middle of this room, but I had to stay focused. The Blood Rite was still the most important thing to me.

Eric and Larissa led the way into the room, Fang bringing up the rear. With my Other sight, I could see the aura of the cast member in the corner of the room. It was vibrant orange, and I had no doubt this was a teen witch. My nerves skyrocketed. If the entire high school theater group was witches, and they'd put on this haunted house... Things were about to get real fucked up.

"Oh, hell no," Larissa shouted, shadows flying off of her at the teenager hovering near her shoulder. They had no way to prepare for the impact of her shadows wrapping around them. "Child don't play with me. Let us pass."

A choking sound left the kid, but the fog lifted enough for us to see the open doorway out of the room. I pushed forward, dragging Jacob with me. Once we had all filed back into the hallway, the door slammed shut. I heard a groan on the other side, glad that the kid was still alive. They deserved the scare for doing this to humans. Where the hell were their parents?

"That was lame. Last year was way better than this." Jacob complained but continued to drag me down the hallway. My brain raced to think of a plan to get out of here before something went horribly wrong. Larissa had tipped us off as witches, the teens may try to prank us even harder to avenge their friend.

"Yeah dude, it shouldn't have been that easy to get out of the—" A shadowy hand appeared over Eric's mouth before he could continue speaking. A show of sparks flashed in our eyes, causing all of us to move back in shock.

Jacob was the first to recover and he shouted, "Oh shit bro! That was awesome."

I sighed before I could stop myself, "I don't like it here. Is there a back way out?"

"Ah, poor Bambi. The haunted house won't hurt you. I'll protect you." He pulled me against his chest, forcing me to breathe in his heavy cologne.

I pulled away coughing, but recovered quickly, "I just wanna go. Surely, we could go find somewhere quiet."

"There isn't a back way out." Fang growled behind us, "That's part of the attraction."

"Let's just keep going then." I said, stomping ahead.

"Plus, now we've got to find Eric." Jacob reminded us. I didn't really care what happened to his friend as he wasn't an innocent human, but it would be best to keep them from killing the guy.

We continued forward, until we found another open door. The room was dark, I didn't complain when Fang pushed to the front of the group and went in first. I followed after, glancing around hoping to spot any auras that might be in the room. It seemed empty, but I had no doubt something was in here with us. I kept walking forward, trying to feel around for a way out. I heard a strange click, before I was yanked off my feet. Seconds later a large glowing anvil came crashing down where I'd been standing. The glow from the anvil lit the room up. Fang held me aloft, having saved me from being crushed by a magic projectile.

"I was going to grab you; he was just closer." Jacob piped up, reminding Fang that we weren't alone.

He sat me back on my feet, "Sorry ma'am. Just didn't want you getting hurt."

"Thanks for the save," I muttered, moving toward Larissa.

"Door is over here." Jacob grunted, looking angry as he pointed to his left. We all had walked right past it.

We filed out of the room in silence, finding ourselves standing in the stairwell. "Up or down?" I asked, baffled. Had they somehow changed the configuration of the house, there was no way this was the real lay out of any home.

"Down." Fang grunted.

"Up." Jacob shot back, "That's what we did last year."

I glanced at Larissa, "Whatever gets us out of here faster." She shrugged.

I sighed, considering the options, "Up isn't going to lead us out. It's possible that there's a basement exit. Some houses have that." I reasoned aloud.

"Down it is." Fang and Larissa said in unison. Jacob didn't speak as we began to take the stairs heading down. My neck prickled, knowing we were being watched, but I couldn't see anyone. Laughs drifted up as we began to approach the bottom of the stairs, causing the hair on my arms to raise in fear. I was afraid of teenagers. I guess I was officially an adult now.

"I'm tired of this shit." Larissa muttered, "Come out you brats. Somebody ought to take a paddle to your behinds." At her words every light around us went out, causing me to stumble. Once again, a firm arm wrapped around my waist, saving me from a tumble down the last few stairs.

"In the old days, witches were burned at the stake," A cacophony of voices echoed all around us, "Let's see if you can survive fire now."

Flames surrounded us, licking far too close for comfort. Jacob yelped in fear, grabbing me tightly. I held in a snort of laughter at his behavior. The flames continued to move closer until we were held in a tight circle, sweat dripping down my back.

"This isn't fucking funny." Fang shouted. "You kids need—"A squelching thud stopped his words. I turned, gasping as Eric's mutilated body came into view. Jacob screamed, rushing toward his friend. Fang stopped him just before flames completely consumed him.

"What the fuck. What the actual fuck is going on?" Jacob screamed, "Where is Eric?"

"Dead." Larissa said, glancing toward me, "Do you think…" She trailed off. I could read her mind; these kids were trying to form a coven on Halloween night. It wasn't unheard of, but they were all far too young. They didn't have the maturity or control to handle the amount of power they were playing with.

Jacob continued to shout and sob in panic. I tuned him out, trying to figure out how we could get out of this situation.

"Would you shut the fuck up." Fang growled at Jacob, "You're bellowing isn't going to get us out of this basement." His words did nothing to stop the guy from continuing to melt down.

I turned around, raising my hand and slapping Jacob in the face, "Stop. Shut up. I can't think with you acting like this."

"You fucking bitch." He lunged toward me, a hand grabbing at my throat. Before he made contact Fang was there.

"That isn't how you speak to a lady." He growled, lifting Jacob off of his feet, "I'm tired of you." He added just before throwing Jacob directly into the flames. The three of us stood in silence as his screams filled the air. A tear rolled down my face, I was never going to complete the Blood Rite now.

Anger bubbled into my chest, causing me to stomp my foot down, "Enough." I held up my hand, willing my magic to extinguish the flames. My power was a wave through the basement, everything it touched turning red before returning to its original state. Without the teenage magic filling the space, the basement was perfectly normal.

"Impressive." Fang muttered.

I ignored him as I noticed seven auras standing behind a door a few feet away. I stomped over, throwing it open. Larissa's shadows flowed around me, gripping the kids and dragging them from the room. I took them in, not one of them looked older than sixteen. Acne and braces graced several of their faces, but they stared at us with no fear. "What are you going to do to us now?" A purple haired girl asked defiantly.

To my surprise, Fang spoke first, "I'm going to report y'all to the Hex Guard. You've already managed to form your coven at this point, but what you've done is completely against our laws. You'll answer for that the way any witch would."

"But it was fucking awesome." One of the guys said, "You gotta admit, we scared you."

I rolled my eyes, "We don't torture and kill innocent humans. You risked breaking innocent human minds. You're lucky you only managed to kill these two."

"We're also calling your parents." Larissa said, her phone held aloft.

"We're not going to give you our names or their numbers." One kid snarled.

"Okay Harry Plont, I'm sure your mother will not be happy about what you've done here." The kid paled as Larissa spoke his name, but she didn't stop, "Melissa Alden, Ryan Burrow, Tabitha Xavier, Penny Philips, Samantha Ellis, and Benny Washington."

The kids all started speaking at the same time, begging her for mercy. I could see the smile pulling at her lips, but she remained serious, "No, you chose to do this. Planned it out. You'll enjoy the consequences of your actions." She turned to Fang and me, "Bambi, get out of here, you're down to just barely four hours until you have to get the Rite done."

"Are you sure you can handle them alone?" I asked.

"Please, Cher. I've dealt with far worse than a few teenage witches." She waved me off.

Fang led me toward the back door that had appeared when their magic had faded. "My truck is just around the block— "

"I have to go find a victim. I can't go with you." I said, crossing my arms.

He sighed, "I know that. If you'll give me just a bit of trust, I'm trying to help you."

"How?" I insisted.

"There's a very well-known house party about a mile up the road. I know some of the people that go. You won't have any issue finding a victim there." He explained. I was too stunned to respond. It was so kind of him that I didn't know what to say. "It's okay to say thank you, Bambi."

"Maybe I misjudged you." I offered instead.

"Close enough." He smiled, leading me away from the house.

Eight

October 31st
8:10PM

Fang had escorted me into the party, nodding to some warlocks that waved to him as we entered. When I turned to thank him, he had disappeared into the crowd. I glanced around the room, looking for humans that might fall for my tricks. I was overwhelmed by the sheer number of oil slicked auras surrounding me. I took a deep breath, settling my nerves. Tonight, I was going to complete the Blood Rite and take my rightful place in the Blood Coven. Soon I would be Priestess, everything I had ever dreamed of was within my reach.

Fang

I watched in rapt attention as Bambi charmed every man within fifty feet of her, human and warlock alike flocked to her. Listening as she told stories and joked. She sat on the kitchen island, her long legs crossed. Every once in a while, she's switched her legs, giving everyone a very brief glimpse of her bare pussy. It was perfect seduction. I was impressed, if she didn't have her heart set on joining the Blood Coven, she'd be a perfect fit in the Black coven. Bambi Crour was sex embodied, even her magic instinctually responded to mine. I'd never done a more powerful ritual than I had that morning after our tryst.

"I'm surprised you came." A deep voice spoke to my left, drawing my attention away from her. "Not really your scene and you've already completed your ritual for the coven." I glanced up to my friend and the Priest of the Black coven, Markus.

"I'm just helping out a friend." I muttered. I liked Markus, we had been friends in school, but he had tricked me into joining his coven not long after my twenty fifth birthday. Regardless of his trickery, we had a friendship that I valued.

"The Blood witch? She is a pretty little thing." I didn't like the way his eyes scanned over her body, "Why help her?"

"She was the person who helped me complete my ritual." I gave him a nonanswer.

"You like her." He observed. I hated that it was so obvious, but Markus knew me better than anyone else on this planet.

I grunted in response, continuing my observation of Bambi's seduction. She had her pick of victims, and I needed to see who she would choose. I wasn't sure why, but it would give me more insight into her mind. I wanted to know everything about her. I'd spent the entire day stalking her around town, learning everything I could about her. She was caring, funny, and probably the hottest woman I'd ever laid eyes on. The moment I'd seen her walking down the road nude, I should have known I was a goner. The way her grey eyes lit up when I'd offered to help her had gone straight to my cock. "Would you let me leave the coven?"

Markus breathed in sharply, "For her? You only met her this morning!"

"Just answer the question." I growled. I didn't need his judgement, when I decided I wanted something I went after it. Bambi wasn't going to leave her coven, so I would have to if we were going to be together. And we would be together.

"Not yet. If you're going to leave for her, I want you to wait until you know her better. She could be a raging bitch; the pretty ones usually are." He said, causing me to crush the can I was holding. No one would talk about Bambi like that; she was going to live a beautiful life if I had to kill everyone who even thought badly of her.

"I can deal with that." I said, trying not to seem as obsessed with her as I truly was.

"What do you know about the Blood Coven?" Markus asked. I shrugged in response, I didn't spend much time looking into other covens, "Eileen Cruor is one bad witch, Fang. She is well known for slaughtering anyone who poses a threat to her people. My guess is that the pretty little girl that's managed to get you wrapped around her finger is the elusive granddaughter of Priestess Cruor. She hasn't been seen at any meetings because her grandmother has hidden her well. She will be the next Priestess."

He was right of course, though I'd learned more in that moment than I had from her all day. Bambi was definitely powerful, I couldn't deny that, but knowing she was in line to become a Priestess... She would always be in danger. My resolve hardened. I would become whatever she needed me to be, but Bambi was now my entire world. I met Markus' eyes, and he must have seen my decision, because he sighed, "I always knew you'd leave us eventually. Never would have guessed it'd be for a woman though."

He was right, this was nothing like me. I didn't care about women, sex, or love. The only thing that had mattered to me for years was growing my power, becoming just as powerful as a Priest without any of the responsibilities. That would serve me well at Bambi's side. I could give her everything she could want and more.

"Looks like your lady has caught the attention of someone you hate." Markus said, drawing my attention back to her. Of course, Cody Demario would show up tonight, he was one of the few humans that knew he was surrounded by witches. I'd hated him ever since he'd backed into my truck, and then claimed it was my fault. It had cost me a pretty penny to have the body damage fixed. I had considered cursing him, but Markus had claimed we needed him. He was a police officer, so he was able to help us out if things got out of hand with a human during a ritual.

I watched as Bambi took him in, her eyes narrowing as he moved close enough to touch her leg. In Other sight, I watched as her red tipped fingers trailed over his hand. Her magic gently testing his aura. Whatever she'd found a smile curled over her lips. She hopped down from the counter, allowing Cody to lead her away from the crowd.

"Are you going to let her go with him?" Markus asked, a strange look on his face. I should stop Bambi from killing him, but I just couldn't seem to make my feet move. My heart warmed, it was almost like she knew exactly who I'd wanted her to choose.

"She's a grown woman; I don't need to make her decisions for her." I responded, hiding my smile. I was going to have the best night of my life. All thanks to the woman I had become obsessed with.

Nine

Bambi
October 31st
10:10PM

Everything was going to plan. The man leading me up the stairs, Cody I think, had the worst aura I'd ever seen. Not an ounce of white could be found around him. He would be perfect for the Rite. I didn't know exactly how I was going to get him away from this house, the warlock's downstairs wouldn't take well to me killing one of their toys. He opened a bedroom door, allowing me to step inside first. He shut the door and immediately stepped into my personal space. The liquor on his breath filled my nose, causing me to sniff. He bent slightly, aiming to press his lips to mine, but I stopped him, "Don't you know somewhere more private? You wouldn't want anyone hearing my noises, would you?" I ran a hand down his chest, aiming for his waist band.

He groaned, "I know a place, but I don't know if I can wait that long."

"I'll make it worth your while," I said, reaching my hand down to cup him through his pants. He wasn't an impressive size, but that didn't matter to me. I hoped to never actually have to come anywhere near his dick.

"I know you will," He groaned, before gripping my arms and pressing his lips to mine. I forced myself to relax, allowing him to slip his tongue in my mouth even as I wanted to gag. We kissed for several minutes, his hands roaming over my clothes before he finally pulled away. "Let's go."

I smiled and allowed him to lead me out of the room. Just before we left, I caught Fang's eye. He had stayed out of my sight most of the night, but I made sure to give him a wink as Cody yanked me out of the house. I knew I'd be seeing him again very soon, the heat in his eyes spurred me on. Maybe I could get one more good birthday fuck.

Thankfully the drive wherever he was taking us wasn't very far. I didn't know how long I could have put up with his roving hands, getting closer and closer to my bare pussy. I didn't know how the Black coven slept with their prey; I couldn't do it. I'd have to ask Fang about that, how he managed to keep it up if his prey wasn't to his tastes. It had to make the spell weaker. A strange moment of jealousy speared me as I imagined Fang with another woman. I shook it off, warmth in my cheeks. I couldn't feel possessive of a man that had stalked me all day, had tricked me into sleeping with him twice. Fuck the sex was good though, I didn't regret it a bit.

"We're here. I know it isn't— "

"It's perfect." I interrupted, patting Cody's leg. The house before us was clearly abandoned, it was far more shack than home at this point. I doubted anyone would come looking here. I let him lead me inside, making sure to take note of the exits in case anything went wrong. Within moments of the door closing behind us, he was on me. Nibbling at my neck, pulling at my dress, little grunts as he gripped my ass hard.

I took a deep breath, murmuring a binding spell, "What did you-"Before he could finish, he flew off of me, his hands bound by invisible string holding him off the ground. "Goddamn it, a fucking witch." I raised an eyebrow, but didn't respond as I hunted around for something sharp. I found a pair of scissors in a drawer, I held my wrist aloft, dragging one of the blades down my arm until blood started to drip. I rushed over to Cody circling him allowing my blood to form a circle around us. "You crazy fucking cunt. Let me go right now, I have powerful friends. People will come looking for me."

"There won't be anything to find." I muttered as the circle was completed. I could feel the energy in my blood vibrating. At that he started to scream and flail, but I ignored him. I broke the scissors, turning them into two separate blades. It wasn't the best weapon to use, but it would do the job. I began to chant the first half of the ritual, "Mother hear me. Father join me. The veil is thin this eve," I paused, trying to remember the exact words, "Take my sacrifice as a sign of my desire to strengthen my coven. Grant me your blessings as I begin the witches ascent." At the height of my voice echoing around us I stabbed one of the blades into Cody's side, pulling out quickly causing a spray of blood to hit me in the face. I twirled around him like a ballerina sinking the other blade into his other side, this blood coating my hand. "A cursed mortal soul to feed on is my gift to you on this night. His blood for energy," I moved in front of him, taking in his crying twisted face. I used one blade to slice open his shirt. Then I began to carve into his bare chest, "His screams for your entertainment," I shouted over his howling, "Wash yourselves in the righteousness of his death." I stabbed both blades through his neck, cutting off his screams.

More of his blood covering my body. I realized I'd forgotten to remove my clothes, so I rushed to unzip my ruined costume, tossing it outside the circle. I ran my hand over his bleeding abdomen, using the blood on my fingers to paint symbols onto my own skin. Once I was finished, I kneeled underneath where his body hung bleeding. It was time for the final piece of my Blood Rite. "Mother, Father. I, Bambi Fay Crour, call on you. I seek your acceptance of my role in the Blood Coven. Allow me to join my brothers and sisters in your holy darkness." The room was completely silent for several seconds before a black flame appeared before me, racing toward my body. I forced myself to remain still as it's cold fire crawled over my body, forced my eyes open as I watched it devour the body of the man I'd offered in sacrifice. Pain shot down my spine as the flame climbed toward my head. I didn't move, didn't make a sound until the flame vanished completely.

Then I fell forward into a puddle of blood, panting. My body was alight with energy. My magic was a force underneath my skin, leaking off of me. When I checked in Other sight, I could see the remnant of red in the air around me. I stood, completely soaked in blood, but unbothered. The room was dark, but I felt around until I found a mirror. With my Other sight I could see the crown of red that now graced my brow. I inhaled sharply, it was the same crown that graced Grandmama's brow.

"He's gone right?" I let out a scream, whirling around to fight off my attacker. Fang stood a few feet away. "No one will be able to find his body?"

"The Mother and Father have him now." I said, a grin spreading across my face. "Do you like my new look." I purred.

"It's certainly impressive." He responded, "I know what that means." Fang motioned toward my head.

"I'm the next Priestess, chosen by them." I confirmed. "What are you doing here?"

"I'm here for you." He replied, moving toward me.

I sighed, "I was afraid of that. You know we can't see each other again."

"That's not true. A Priestess may not collude with non-coven warlocks, but they can initiate new members." Fang said as he finally was close enough to touch me. "I have to admit, I thought the blood would be a turn off, but seeing you like this... I only want you more."

I didn't have a response to that. I knew what he was saying, he was going to leave his coven to be with me. It was crazy, I knew that, but something about it made me want him desperately. I didn't hesitate to close the space between us, reaching up to pull his lips to mine. His hands slipped over my waist, smearing the blood coating me. "Inside me, now." I groaned as his hands wrapped into my hair. He glanced around the room, noticing the circle coated in blood. He pulled me over, pushing me to my knees. I waited patiently as he stripped all of his clothes out. When he returned, I ran my bloody hands over his hard stomach and thighs, coating him in blood as well, "Might as well get used to it now."

Fang laughed, "Whatever I need to do to get inside that sweet pussy right now." His eyes darkened, his demeanor changing as he gripped my hair again, "Why don't you get that ass up in the air for me. I haven't taken you that way yet."

I scrambled to turn around, pushing my ass into the air as I pressed my chest into the hardwood floor. Fang groaned but kneeled behind me. He kneaded my ass, causing me to moan. "Think you can make me cum a third time today, Bambi?"

"Of course I can." I huffed.

He chuckled before grabbing my hips and slamming to the hilt into me. I screamed as he did it again, causing me to lurch forward. His pace was punishing, his hips grinding into me hard as he took me unlike any of the other times. I could almost feel him claiming me, so I began to return his strokes. Taking him deeply, begging for more. I had no idea how much time passed as we became one, spiraling faster and faster toward the finish line. I was shaking, barely holding off my orgasm when Fang pulled me into his chest. "Who do you belong to?"

"You." I panted, "I belong to you."

Fang shuttered as his orgasm spilled into me, "And I'm yours now too." With all the sensations I couldn't hold it off any longer. Wave after wave of pleasure crashed over me. Leaving us a shaking mess in the floor, covered in another man's blood. We laid there for a long time, not speaking, soaking in each others warmth.

"We need to clean this mess up." Fang pointed out.

"I need to get back home." I said, sitting up. "Grandmama will have felt my Rite completion. She'll be expecting me."

"I'm going with you." He insisted.

My eyes widened, "Absolutely not. I'll need to prepare her to be introduced to you. Grandmama is not welcoming to strangers."

"I'm not going to be a stranger for long. I'll be joining her coven very, very soon." He argued. Before I could open my mouth to argue, "Come on. You're not going to win this one."

"Will I ever win any of them?" I sassed.

"Sometimes." He shot back, "Just not yet." I rolled my eyes, but decided to let him drive me home. I still hadn't figured out exactly how far away I was. I could use my newly acquired power, but the humor of seeing Fang and Grandmama in the same room was going to be too good to miss.

Ten

November 1st

12:34AM

"Bambi Cruor, you cut it awfully close today." Grandmama's disapproving voice welcomed me home.

"Don't I know it." I shot back, "Grandmama, I have someone to intro-"

"Bring the man inside, Bambi. As if I don't know when another warlock steps foot onto my territory. Fang Boucher what brings you here?" She asked.

I should have known she'd be a step ahead of us, "Thanks for inviting me in, ma'am. I wanted to introduce myself since I'll be your grandson in law soon enough."

I gasped at his words, "Woah now. I never agreed-"

"I approve. She is the next Priestess of this coven, that makes you the next Priest. Are you prepared for that?" Grandmama nodded.

"What?!" I shouted.

"I have been training my magic for almost twelve years ma'am." Fang responded.

"Wait how old are you?" I interrupted him.

"I'm thirty-seven, Bambi." He said, patting my shoulder gently, "Markus Withersby is my current Priest. He has insisted on some time before he'll allow me to leave the Black coven."

"We'll see about that." Grandmama said, lifting herself from her chair. Her grey hair was clipped high on her head, a blue dressing gown hiding her body. She picked up her cell phone. After a few rings a male's voice came through the other end, "Yes, Markus. Just making a courtesy call, Fang Boucher is joining my coven." Markus' voice picked up pitch as he spoke quickly, "I understand it's short notice... Mhm mhm. No, I don't care how long they've known each other." She paused for a moment, pressing fingers to her forehead, "Lord, boy. You'd think you weren't a warlock. When a witch and warlock are meant for one another, nothing will keep them apart. Have you seen their auras?"

That caused me to switch to Other sight. I glanced to Fang, shocked to find a red hue slowly overtaking his aura. "I'll send him home tonight, but when you see what I'm seeing I think you'll agree with me. We wouldn't want to anger the Mother and Father." She smirked as she disconnected the call. "Come. Sit. Bambi hasn't been informed on witch bonds yet." Grandmama said to Fang.

"Witch bonds?" I echoed, allowing Fang to lead me to the couch.

"I didn't expect it to come up so young for you. Most witches don't form a witch bond until they're well into their thirties or even forties. It's a very serious commitment." She explained, "Witch bonds cannot be broken. They form when two compatible witches perform a ritual together."

"Wait. You mean this morning?" I glanced at Fang, "Did you know that would happen?" I accused him.

"Of course not," He grunted, "I thought witch bonds were rare."

"Is that why you chased me all over town." I whispered. Grandmama laughed, "It's not funny! He's the reason I almost didn't complete the Blood Rite tonight."

Fang held his hands up, "You ran off anytime I tried to talk to you. When you finally explained what you were doing, I gave you the space to do it."

"Did you know?" I glared at him.

"No, but it makes sense. You've consumed my every waking moment since..." He trailed off, nodding to Grandmama respectfully.

She nodded back, "That's normal. And it seems the Mother and Father have already blessed your union. Fang will need to join the Blood Coven soon, keeping bonded witches apart is against coven law."

"Markus will let me leave." Fang reassured her, "We're longtime friends. Even if he doesn't like it, he won't want to risk a visit from the Hex Guard."

"It won't come to that." Grandmama said, a vague threat underlining her words. "For tonight, you need to leave. Get your affairs settled. Allow me to welcome my granddaughter into our coven properly."

Fang stood, pressing a kiss into my hair, "I'll be back soon."

"Okay." I said, dazed as he exited the house.

"You're tired, but the coven wants to welcome you before you go to bed." Grandmama said, coming to run a hand over my hair.

"I need to clean up first." I was covered in dried blood and only wearing a large flannel that Fang had had in his truck.

"They'll expect you to look like this." She argued, pulling me up, and leading me toward the back door.

I took a deep breath before nodding for her to open the door. I pasted a smile on my face as we stepped out onto the back porch together. The Blood Coven was large, but only about half the coven was here tonight. Several whoops and hollers went up; my name was being chanted. My shoulders relaxed, my smile becoming genuine. I loved my coven. I'd known most of these people my entire life. My success was their success. "Blood Coven witches and warlocks, welcome your newest member, Priestess in training, Bambi Fay Cruor." Claps and continued shouting grew louder.

I gave a sassy courtesy, as I walked through the crowd hugging several people. Letting them take in my blood covered body, "I am honored to finally join you. I will be the best witch and Priestess the Mother and Father could want for the Blood coven." I raised my fist in the air, laughing as I yelled. We danced around fires and ate food until the sun began to peak over the horizon.

I was sweaty and exhausted when Grandmama called everyone to heel. I didn't even listen as she gave a quick blessing to the Mother and Father before sending everyone home. Once we were alone I wrapped an arm around her shoulders as we walked into our home, "I'm surprised you didn't make Fang stay for the celebration."

"This was your night, Bambi. No one else deserved a moment of their attention but you." She responded, "Now I'm taking these weary old bones to bed."

"Goodnight, Grams." I said, as I yawned. I collapsed into my childhood bed, a sigh of happiness filling the room. My twenty fifth birthday had been perfect.

Epilogue

I t had taken two weeks to align all of our plans. Markus had given more push back than Grandmama expected, but ultimately the power of the witch bond and the laws surrounding it won. Fang was still in the process of selling his home so he could move closer to me. Next week we would start house shopping. I refused to stay in Grandmama's home a moment longer than absolutely necessary. The idea of her overhearing our... activities made my stomach roll. Anytime Fang and I were together we couldn't help ourselves; I needed that man's dick like I needed air in my lungs. My magic nearly bursting out of my chest to get to his whenever we were connected.

"Get out of your head, girl. This is basically your wedding ceremony." Larissa said, bumping her hip into mine.

"Isn't that normal? Getting married to someone I've only known for a few weeks is insane." I pointed out.

"It's different with a witch bond." Grandmama's voice startled me. I turned toward her, taking in the black robe that she was wearing. Her red crown of her magic was on full display, shining against her grey hair. She looked every bit the Priestess that she was. "If you don't want to go through with it today, we will postpone."

"I can't make the coven wait." I sighed, "And it's not that Fang isn't the man that I want. It just feels so sudden, I've only been ascended for a couple of weeks."

"You'll have plenty of time to train your powers before you take my place. I'm not ready to give up being Priestess just yet." Grandmama responded, "Fang Boucher is a good man, underneath all that gruff he hides behind."

"I know." I responded, smoothing the silk of my red dress as I sat. "I even think that I'm falling in love with him."

"Then you will complete your witch bond before the coven today. Fang will be a member of the Blood Coven, and you will be Priest and Priestess in training." Larissa said. "Everything else will come with time."

"Listen to her, Bambi. Don't deny yourself happiness out of fear. I've raised you better than that." Grandmama added, before she produced a velvet box from thin air. Her power was far more advance than any other witch I'd ever seen, I still had so much to learn from her. "This was my mother's and her mother's before that. It has been passed down to each of the women in the Cruor family for generations. Today you will wear it so that they may smile down upon us from their place with the Mother and Father." She opened the box, revealed a silver chain with a giant red ruby dangling from it.

I gasped, pulling the pendant into my hand. "It's beautiful."

"Not as beautiful as you." She said, pressing a kiss to the top of my head, "I know I've been hard on you most of your life, Bambi, but you are the light in my heart. You have exceeded my expectations again and again. There is no one else that I would hand control of the Blood Coven to." Tears filled my eyes as she added, "When you're ready."

"I love you." I said, standing to throw my arms around her. She clasped the chain around my neck, the ruby was heavier than I expected, but it laid perfectly between my breasts. As I stared into the mirror, I saw a flash of the Priestess I would one day become. Strong and powerful, not just because of the power I held, but because of the amazing woman who had raised me when my parents died.

"And I you." She responded, "It's time. Let's bring Fang into the family."

Larissa left, joining the coven before I made my entrance. I looped my arm with Grandmama's before we began our trek to the outdoor platform that had been erected yesterday. In many ways this was set up in the same way a human wedding would be. An arch of black and red roses awaited at the end of the aisle. The entire coven was in attendance as Grandmama and I made our way to the platform, they tossed various items in the pathway, shouting their blessings. I noticed a finger bone hit my bare foot, and I nearly snorted aloud. We were a macabre bunch. I guess that came with being Blood Witches.

Finally, I met Fang's hazel eyes. He stood in a simple all black outfit that was tight against his musclar body, his red hair and beard had been trimmed. A smirk curled up his lip as we took each other in. He knew what the ritual consisted of, could probably tell the lust that pulsed through me as I'd perused his body. When Grandmama and I finally made it to him, she released my hand, placing it in his. "Hello, brothers and sisters." Her voice boomed out over the crowd, silencing their shouts, "We are gathered here for a twofold reason this evening. First, Fang Boucher is here to join the Blood Coven. And it is time that Fang and Bambi are bound before the eyes of the coven." She held up a hand as the crowd shouted their praise. It wasn't often that a new warlock joined the coven, much less due to a witch bond. "Fang Boucher, it is my duty to swear you into the coven. Are you ready to serve the Blood Coven as we follow the path the Mother and Father have laid out for us?"

"I am." He responded.

"Then repeat after me." Grandmama said, before their voices became entwined.

"The seven laws of the Mother and Father guide our way. Our powers are gifted to us to use as they see fit. I will honor them before all else. The bonds of the Coven are sacred; I shall not break them. Blood, I sacrifice to join, Blood I will bathe in until the day I am returned to the arms of the Mother." As Fang finished the final line, Grandmama pulled an athame from her robe, slashing open his palm. His blood dripped into a vial that Grandmama held, once the vial was full, she tucked it into her robe. I watched in Other Sight as Fang's pink magic morphed to the same deep red as mine. He would still be able to use sex magic, but now he would be recognized as a Blood warlock as well. Shouts and claps sounded as the ritual was completed. I held my breath realizing it was time for our bonding.

Grandmama quieted the crowd, "Now Bambi Cruor shall be bound to Fang Boucher before the coven. Their witch bond is strong and blessed by the Mother and Father, may we bask in their love today."

Fang leaned in close, clearly sensing my anxiety, "They will only see what you want them to see."

I nodded, gathering my courage as Grandmama said, "Bertrum, bring the brands."

My heart skipped a beat as the old gardener appeared with two small metal rods. Even knowing what was coming didn't ease the tension of the moment. Fang began unbuttoning his shirt as Grandmama produced a mason jar of red liquid from her robes.

I was convinced she'd done some kind of spell on her robes that allowed her to hide anything in them, but she refused to give me that information. The woman loved to be mysterious. "This blood was saved from the first kill of my daughter, Barbie. Though she has long been passed on to the Mother, today she'll join us in spirit as her daughter completes her witch bond." Tears sprang to my eyes at the mention of my mother. We didn't speak of her often. It was too hard on both of us. My mother was killed by my father, who was then executed by the Hex Guard. To this day we don't know the details of that night. Grandmama took me in and raised me as her own. Fang, noticing my emotions, grabbed my hand giving it a squeeze.

I took a deep breath, reaching around to unzip my beautiful dress. Being naked in front of the coven wasn't the part of this that made me nervous, so when my dress pooled around my feet, I stepped closer to Fang, allowing the heat of his body to warm me. We turned toward Grandmama as she opened the jar of sacred blood, carefully dipping each rod into it. Once both were soaked in blood, they were handed to us. We both held them in our right hands, joined at our left hands. It was silent as we used our magic to heat the tip of the brand, once it glowed a fiery red, we turned toward each other.

"You first," Fang whispered, squaring his shoulders, "Right over my heart, so you will always be close to what you own." I pressed the glowing metal into his pectoral, right above his heart. He didn't flinch as his skin smoked from the brand. When I pulled it away a crescent moon shape was left in its place. It was a dark red and would remain that way after healing, assisted by magic. "Turn around." He instructed, keeping hold of my hand as I faced the crowd. He leaned in close to my ear, "I want to see my mark every time I have you bent over for me." With those words he pressed the brand into the center of my lower back. I released air through my teeth, but didn't move as I felt the magic seep into my skin. I wasn't prepared for the purple light that engulfed us as Fang tossed the brand away. He turned me, lifting me into his arms as his lips crashed down on mine. I could hear Grandmama trying to calm the coven as they shouted and celebrated. Purple was the color of the Mother and Father, as my mind focused on Fang, I realized that the first time we were together purple light had shown when he'd completed his spell. Our union was truly blessed by the gods of witches.

"Go, enjoy your time together in private." Grandmama said, breaking us apart. "This is an occasion for celebration."

Fang didn't gather our clothes as he carried me inside. At this point he'd learned the way to my room, dropping me unceremoniously onto the bed. "You are mine." He growled.

"I was from the moment I climbed into your truck." I responded.

We didn't speak another word as he took me in every way, he knew I loved to be taken. The sounds of the Coven celebrating our blessed union covered the sounds that we made as we found our pleasure over and over again. When the sun began to peak through the curtains we separated, panting and sated. Fang fell asleep, wrapped around me as if I was the most precious treasure in the world. I stared at the ceiling of my childhood bedroom for a long time, sending my thanks to the Mother and Father for all that they had blessed me with. When I finally drifted off to sleep, I dreamed of red headed children with my grey eyes, of the Priest's crown upon our brows, and of all the love I had found on Halloween night.